MW01504316

TERRORISM
The New Menace

Keith Greenberg

THE MILLBROOK PRESS
Brookfield, Connecticut

Published by The Millbrook Press
2 Old New Milford Road
Brookfield, CT 06804
© 1994 Blackbirch Graphics, Inc.

5 4 3 2 1

Created and produced in association with Blackbirch Graphics.
Series Editor: Bruce S. Glassman

Library of Congress Cataloging-in-Publication Data
Greenberg, Keith, 1959–
    Terrorism: the new menace / by Keith Greenberg.
        p.   cm. — (Headliners)
    Includes bibliographical references and index.
    Summary: This book investigates the increase in terrorist activity in the
United States. It reports and interprets such events as the World Trade Center
bombing. It considers the history of terrorism, how it can be prevented, and
what it means for the future.
    ISBN 1-56294-488-6
    1. Terrorism—Juvenile literature. 2. Terrorism—United States—Juvenile
literature. [Terrorism.] I. Title. II. Series.
HV6431.G726   1994
303.6'25'0973—dc20   93-23565
                                                                     CIP
                                                                      AC

√   3469700019854

Contents

Chapter 1

The Menace Strikes Home

It was a typical Friday in the busy offices of the World Trade Center in New York City. Executives, mail room clerks, and secretaries in the center's Twin Towers—the two tallest buildings in the city—were looking forward to the weekend. In the morning, people made telephone calls, arranging to have lunch with friends working in nearby offices. Others were too busy to eat out. They had meals delivered by the many Chinese restaurants, pizza parlors, and sandwich shops in the area.

Lunch hour started without incident. Conversations centered around vacation plans, engagements, and problems on the job. It was unlikely that anyone suspected the World Trade Center would be the target of a terrorist attack. Yet that was exactly what was about to happen.

At 12:18 p.m. that February 26, 1993, Gina, a legal secretary from Brooklyn, was at her desk on the fortieth floor of Two World Trade Center, making a telephone call. She dialed and heard the other line ring. Then the lights flickered and the phone suddenly went dead. "We felt the building moving," she recalled later, "like an earthquake." Still, Gina was not alarmed. It was probably an electrical problem of some sort; the lights will come on in a little while, she told herself.

On February 26, 1993, a giant explosion rocked New York's World Trade Center.

Opposite:
Two police officers help a woman who was injured in the World Trade Center blast.

The bomb went off in the parking garage underground, destroying a train station and seriously weakening the foundation and structural supports of Two World Trade Center.

But forty floors down, people were not as calm. A huge explosion had torn through the underground parking garage of the Twin Towers and the large neighboring New York Vista Hotel, blasting a hole through three levels of concrete. Pillars collapsed. Cars were flattened. Other autos lay on their sides, lights blinking and alarms blaring. "This explosion is so bad, you'd almost need another bomb to straighten the mess out again," one rescue worker said while looking at the damage.

Power in the buildings was out. Water pipes had burst open. Elevators were trapped between floors, stranding passengers for hours.

Robert Kirkpatrick had been a supervisor in charge of locksmithing and carpentry at the World Trade Center for ten years. Friends knew him as a man who could fix anything. At sixty-one years old, he was looking forward to retiring in nine months and traveling with his wife. Generally, he never ate lunch in his office near the parking garage. But, today, for some reason, he had. Now, Robert was dead, along with five others: secretary Monica Smith, who was five months pregnant with her first child; John DiGiovanni, a salesman who was parking his car in the garage at the time of the explosion; Wilfredo Mercado, a purchasing agent for the New York Vista Hotel; Steve Knapp and William Macko, both of whom oversaw the heating, air conditioning, and refrigeration in the one-hundred-ten-story towers. The pair had recently received medals for bravery for rescuing a person caught in a fire. Additionally, 1,042 people were injured.

Up on the fortieth floor, Gina was unaware of the chaos below. But when she looked out her window, she heard sirens and saw hundreds of people rushing out of the building. After some discussion, she and the other workers decided to leave.

The hallway was filled with smoke. "You could see through it," Gina remembered, "but it was getting thicker." She and five companions began slowly walking down the dark staircase, with thousands of other workers. Unable to see, they grasped the banister and searched for each step ahead of them with their feet. "We still didn't understand how serious this was," Gina said. "The whole way down, we were joking around."

Others were not so cheerful. One pregnant woman went into seizures. Medics and a firefighter carried her down thirty-four flights of stairs and rushed her to the nearest hospital, where she gave birth. Another pregnant woman and five others had to be rescued by helicopter from the observation deck thousands of feet above the city at the top of Two World Trade Center.

When she finally made it outside, Gina saw people in business suits, covered with soot. There were long lines at pay phones, as survivors tried to call relatives and tell them everything was fine. She looked up and saw curtains flapping in the wind through a broken window in the glass-fronted towers. A helicopter hovered overhead. Then she told herself, "I think this is worse than I thought."

The rest of the country was just as surprised as Gina was when she learned the explosion was the work of terrorists. Yes, New York City had experienced smaller bombings by groups dedicated to everything from freedom for Soviet Jews to independence for Puerto Rico. But nothing had ever been waged on such a huge level. In the past, terrorism of this magnitude had been a plague that only people in Europe and the Middle East had to worry about. With the bombing of the World Trade Center, terrorists had extended their arena to American soil.

"The terrorists have finally infiltrated the United States," said Christopher Abbate, a volunteer with the American Red Cross, as he helped victims outside the World Trade Center. "We may be the strongest country in the world, yet we're so vulnerable."

In the days after the explosion, a variety of individuals called authorities, claiming to know the identity of the culprits. Among the groups named were Croatian, Bosnian, and Serbian terrorists from the former Yugoslavia, and Colombian drug barons. Authorities went to work immediately to establish who was *really* responsible.

Investigating

By March 1, certain details about the bombing were beginning to fall into place. Authorities determined that the explosive had been transported into the World Trade Center garage in a large car or van. They examined tapes from two surveillance cameras in the garage. Investigators also studied a videotape of the area shot by a tourist.

Opposite:
Agents from the U.S. Bureau of Alcohol, Tobacco, and Firearms (ATF) search through the rubble for clues underneath Two World Trade Center. Investigators constructed scaffolding to move up and down in the huge crater left by the explosion.

They inspected parking stubs for license plate numbers. Witnesses were questioned about any people who had been behaving suspiciously.

The next day, the remains of ten damaged vehicles were pulled from the garage. The identification number of a van—the only recovered vehicle large enough to have carried the large load of explosives—was traced to a Ryder truck rental office in Jersey City, New Jersey.

The Monday before the bombing, Mohammed Salameh, an Egyptian immigrant, had gone to the office and put down a $400 deposit to rent a truck. After the explosion, he reported the vehicle stolen and asked for his deposit back. Once FBI agents traced the van to Salameh—and learned about his desire to be repaid—they suspected he was involved with the bombing and came up with a plan. Stationed outside the office, they waited for Salameh to return to collect his money, then arrested him. In Salameh's pocket, authorities reported finding a truck rental contract splattered with traces of chemicals from explosives.

In Salameh's old but well-kept building, tenants were stunned to learn that the FBI believed their quiet neighbor was actually part of a terror ring. Around the country, residents began to wonder which people in *their* towns might secretly be involved in the same type of activities. Even scarier, FBI director William Webster stated that there were "dozens and dozens" of similar organizations around the nation—from a variety of backgrounds— capable of striking at any time.

Officials React

In October 1993, Salameh and three others—Mahmud Abouhalima, Nidal Ayyad, and Ahmad Ajaj—went on trial for the World Trade Center bombing. Prosecutor Gilmore Childers told the court that the suspects tried to "put America on notice," by committing terrorist acts.

Even before the trial public officials were quick to propose safeguards against future terrorism. New York senator Alfonse D'Amato urged other lawmakers to pass a bill making bombing murders punishable by death. "Those guilty of the World Trade Center bombing have the blood of innocent victims on their hands, yet they will have their own lives spared," he said publicly. Later, the FBI would claim the senator's comments provoked the suspects' associates to begin plotting his assassination.

In a public address, President Bill Clinton declared, "The American people should be very proud of the work done by the law enforcement authorities," and "should be very much reassured by the speed with which the law enforcement people responded."

But attorney Edward Bright, whose law firm had to close because of the explosion, told the newspaper *New York Newsday,* "I don't feel particularly relieved. There are a lot of crazies out there, and this will give other people ideas."

The New Terrorism

Terrorism has long been defined as attacks—bombings, hijackings, hostage taking—committed for political purposes. The motivations behind the assaults vary as much as the methods. Members of the Irish Republican Army (IRA) have long attacked British soldiers and planted bombs as a means of ending English control of Northern Ireland. Assassinations by members of India's Sikh minority and Spain's Basques are seen by supporters as a way of securing independence for these groups.

This is a strategy that has actually worked in the past. The founders of the state of Israel engaged in terrorist activities—such as the bombing of Jerusalem's King David Hotel—to terminate British rule in the Jewish homeland. Ironically, Israel's leaders would later despair when Arabs acted similarly in an effort to form their own state.

But over recent years, terrorism has added a new dimension. There are many more kinds of groups willing to use terrorist tactics to achieve their varied goals. The Soviet Union—sometimes a sponsor of terrorism in the West—dissolved in 1991. Afterward, many long-simmering regional and ethnic conflicts boiled over through terrorism.

In Germany, bombs have been hurled at refugee centers by militants opposed to increased immigration. In Colombia and Italy, members of organized crime have blown up buildings and murdered officials. In America, abortion opponents have bombed clinics and shot doctors, and animal rights extremists have targeted testing laboratories.

Because many of the new terrorists are forming small, independent groups—and are thus harder to identify—fighting terrorism has become more difficult. "We need to improve our capabilities," a U.S. government official told *Time* magazine, "to try to out-think them, to out-imagine them."

But out-thinking terrorists is hard because some terrorist acts that are masterminded by a small group of people may not be planned far in advance. Some militants today take directions from no one but themselves, and they attack on the spur of the moment. Police can't predict where terrorism will occur because the outlaws "don't know in the morning what they will be doing that night," said Ernst Uhrlau, a German law enforcement director.

Traditional Terrorist Techniques

Recent patterns in no way signify the end of old style terrorism in which large, militant, and well-known groups carry out plans that seem to have been carefully planned. In a single day in June 1993, for example, radical members of Turkey's Kurdish minority vented their anger on Turkish embassies, businesses, and banks in twenty-nine cities throughout Europe. While some of the attackers only vandalized the facilities, others were more violent.

Opposite:
Debris and destruction from an IRA bomb blast litter the streets of London's financial district in April 1993. Police estimated that a ton of explosives was used, causing about $300 million in damage.

Training Terrorists for Destruction

During the 1980s, Libya's leader, Colonel Muammar el-Qaddafi, was frequently named as the prime sponsor of terror in the world. In 1986, there were said to be over thirty terrorist training camps in Libya, preparing followers devoted to every cause from Palestinian statehood to Irish independence from England.

One Libyan hit man arrested in Europe gave investigators an insight into the way terrorists were trained. At one particular camp, three courses were underway at the same time. Instructors concentrated on the use of small weapons, some with silencers, and explosives. After six months, assassins were graduated in groups of forty.

The hit man confessed that, after leaving the training camp, he was given a fake Tunisian passport and sent to Europe. There, he would use a pay phone to check in with a commander in Libya. When he was given an order to kill, he could pick up weapons at a local office of the Libyan government by using a code word. After the mission was over, he would leave the scene of the crime by flying home on Libyan Arab Airlines.

Members of the IRA train at a terrorist camp in an undisclosed location.

A total of thirty-one hostages were taken in Munich, Germany, and Marseilles, France. They were then released. In Bern, Switzerland, a Kurd was killed in a confrontation with police.

Funding for this type of activity often comes from international sources. The IRA receives much of its money from Irish Americans who support Irish Independence. Sources worldwide also finance the smaller, less well-known groups whose actions characterize recent terrorism. The World Trade Center conspirators may have been helped by the government of the Sudan, which wants to see all countries in the Middle East turn back toward their Muslim roots and denounce the West, particularly the United States.

Such so-called state-sponsored terrorism has become an increasing concern. By 1993, the United States had placed economic sanctions upon several foreign countries, including Iran, Iraq, and North Korea, for supporting terrorism—and especially terrorist acts aimed at America.

America as a Target

America has long been resented in some countries around the globe. Critics of the U.S. government say it has supported dictators receptive to American companies operating in their countries, or who shared America's dislike of the Soviet Union. With the end of the USSR, America became the world's only superpower—and thus a large target of much of the world's bitterness.

Americans have often been victims of terrorism, but most incidents took place overseas, and little threat was felt on a daily basis. The World Trade Center bombing, however, changed all that. Citizens realized that the United States is still unpopular among many, and terrorists can now operate within the once-safe boundaries of the fifty states.

The menace had struck home. Yet it had a history spanning fifty years throughout the world.

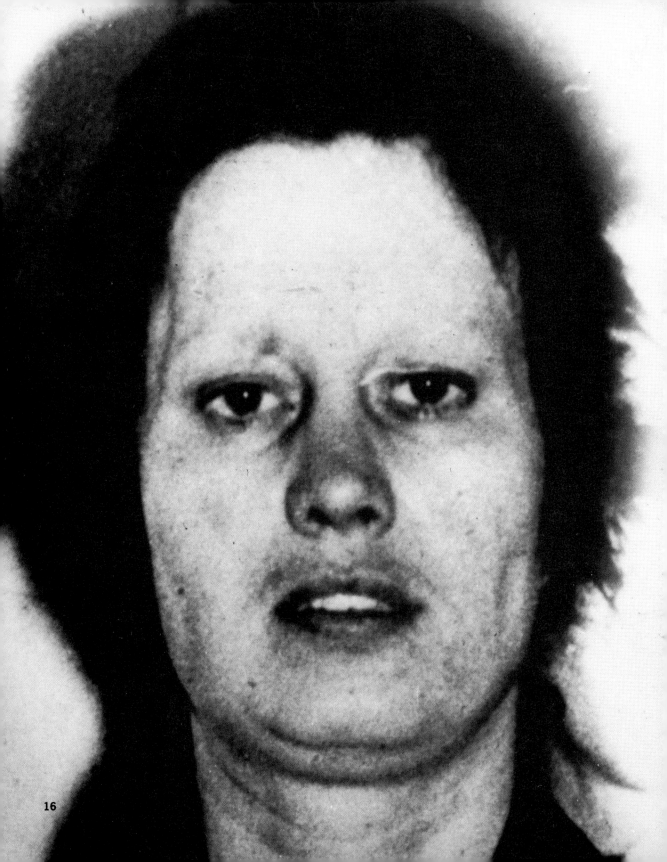

16

Chapter 2

Conspiracies of Fear

When World War II ended, many people clung to the hope that the images of concentration camps and bombed-out cities would linger long enough to deter future wars. But memories of World War II's horrors were not enough to halt humankind from engaging in new wars, as well as creating terrorist organizations all over the world.

Europe's Communist Gangs

Terrorist organizations have traditionally sprouted in such places as France, Portugal, and Belgium, sometimes working with like-minded groups in other countries. Perhaps the best-organized of these factions was Germany's Baader-Meinhof gang. The Baader-Meinhof gang was committed to taking power away from Europe's "ruling class," and fighting American influence everywhere. The movement first gained notoriety in 1970, when a band of supporters—including female journalist Ulrike Meinhof—shot their way into a prison and freed leader Andreas Baader. In 1972, the organization was responsible for fifteen bombings in German cities. Living underground, the gang had a number of five-person units stationed in

Groups have organized in many countries around the world to call attention to their causes through terror.

Opposite:
German terrorist leader Ulrike Meinhof led her gang on a series of bombings and murders in the 1970s.

twenty-five locations in West Germany. In 1977, however, four leaders committed suicide in prison.

But the battles continued elsewhere. The Baader-Meinhof leaders changed the group's name to Red Army Faction to imply that they were one branch of an international communist—or "red," as Soviet supporters were sometimes called—revolution. Declaring the same allegiance to communism, Italy's Red Brigades also emerged.

The Red Brigades specialized in kidnapping prominent business and political leaders, branding them "enemies of the people" and holding special trials—or "people's courts"—to determine guilt. Their most daring escapade took place in March 1978, when a well-trained Red Brigades team swooped down on the car of Aldo Moro, one of Italy's most famous politicians. All five of Moro's bodyguards were killed in the shootout, and the statesman was taken into custody. Moro's captors held him for forty-five days, forcing him to participate in a Red Brigades' "trial" and make statements condemning his former associates. He was finally executed with a machine gun, and his body was dumped in the trunk of a car. The vehicle was purposely left halfway between the headquarters of two political parties opposed to negotiating with the terrorists for Moro's release.

The IRA

The Irish Republican Army—or IRA—is probably the best-known European terrorist organization. Although many sympathize with its cause—uniting the Republic of Ireland with British-ruled Northern Ireland—the IRA's methods are frequently scorned.

All of Ireland was once governed by the British, who discriminated against the Catholic community. There were several uprisings until, in 1922, the country was divided. The twenty-six Catholic counties of southern Ireland would eventually become the Republic of Ireland.

The six counties of Northern Ireland—inhabited mainly by Protestants loyal to England—would remain British.

Catholics continued to be mistreated in Northern Ireland, working at lower-paying jobs and living in inferior housing. The IRA staged bombings and shootings as a means of pressuring England to let go of the six counties. But the world was largely indifferent until 1968, when Catholics rallying against living conditions were attacked by Protestant extremists. On January 30, 1972, British troops fired on a protest, killing 13 men. This day—known as "Bloody Sunday"—became a symbol of British oppression and a rallying point for Catholic wrath against England.

The IRA soon stepped up bombings and assassinations. In 1979, the group shocked all of England by killing Prince Philip's uncle, Earl Mountbatten, by blowing up his fishing boat. That same year, IRA guerillas attacked a British parachute regiment, killing eighteen people. Then in 1984, the organization almost slaughtered English prime minister Margaret Thatcher's entire cabinet when a

The remains of Earl Mountbatten's boat are loaded onto a trailer in Ireland after the British royal was killed in an explosion. The IRA claimed responsibility for the murder.

bomb exploded at a gathering of the ruling Conservative party in the resort town of Brighton. One government minister died. Thatcher and the rest of her cabinet narrowly missed the same fate.

The IRA also goes after non-government targets, planting bombs on busy streets, in department stores, and train stations throughout England. On April 24, 1993, one innocent person was killed and forty-four were injured when an explosion ripped through London's financial district, shattering thousands of windows and shaking sidewalks along dozens of blocks. The IRA's goal is not only to gain publicity for their cause, but to sour the British people on their government's stance in Northern Ireland. If enough English are hurt or inconvenienced, the IRA reasons, they will pressure the administration to pull out of Northern Ireland to prevent further terror.

But the IRA's actions may be having an opposite effect. In March 1993, after an IRA bomb in a British shopping mall killed twelve-year-old Tim Parry and three-year-old Jonathan Ball, a Dublin mother named Susan McHugh started a movement that is dedicated to creating peace in Northern Ireland. The IRA "doesn't kill in the name of Ireland," she said. "Most people here are ashamed of these slaughters."

With both Catholics and Protestants rejecting terrorist activity, there is hope that Northern Ireland's troubles will be resolved through peaceful negotiations in the near future.

America's Radical Outlaws

America has sometimes served as a battleground for people incensed about circumstances in other parts of the world. For many years, the Omega 7 movement—dedicated to the overthrow of Cuban Communist leader Fidel Castro—targeted Cuban Americans accused of being sympathetic to the dictator. Three militant Croatians shot their way into Yugoslavia's mission to the United Nations in New York on June 14, 1977, wounding a chauffeur and taking the ambassador hostage. Before surrendering to police, the intruders demanded Croatia's liberty from Yugoslavia—an event that would finally occur in 1991. Croatian nationalists were also suspected in a 1980 bomb blast at the Statue of Liberty.

Usually, however, terrorism in America was directed against the United States government. The Weathermen, also known as the Weather Underground, considered themselves the leaders of a violent revolution against the American capitalistic system that they believed to be the cause of oppression and poverty in the United States. Noted for bombings, the group had New York City in a state of fear in early 1970. On March 12, three separate bombs damaged office buildings in busy Manhattan. Ten days later, fifteen people were injured in a dance floor

A number of explosions that destroyed buildings in New York City were attributed to the Weather Underground in 1970. This brownstone in Greenwich Village supposedly housed a homemade bomb factory with several bombs and nearly sixty sticks of dynamite.

explosion in a night club. On March 28, three members of the Weathermen were killed in two blasts in a house containing fifty-seven sticks of dynamite and several bombs.

Two of the survivors went into hiding, and the organization was forced to operate in secrecy. In 1980, when three Weather Underground fugitives turned themselves in, many believed the movement was finished. But one year later, the May 19 Communist Organization—related to the Weathermen—received national attention when three members killed two policemen and a guard in an attempted armored car robbery in Nanuet, New York.

Organizations, like Los Macheteros and FALN (Frente Armado por Liberacion Nacional; translated—Armed Front for National Liberation), engaged in a number of terrorist activities in American cities to pressure the United

Rescue workers at New York's La Guardia Airport search for survivors through the wreckage of a bomb blast in December 1975. Twelve people were killed and about 35 others were injured in the explosion.

States to grant Puerto Rico its independence. The FALN was the prime suspect in a bombing at New York's La Guardia Airport that killed twelve on December 29, 1975.

The Palestinian Problem

In the Arab world, the United States—a steadfast supporter of Israel—has been largely blamed for the problems that Palestinians have in Israel. As a result, American locations around the world have often been targeted by terrorist groups sympathetic to the Palestinian cause.

In the past, Palestinian Arabs—both Muslim and Christian—had long lived in what is now the state of Israel, governed by England until after World War II. When the war ended, European Jewish refugees from the Nazi death camps flooded the country—then called Palestine—demanding their own homeland. These immigrants often settled in areas that had been exclusively Palestinian. In 1947, the newly formed United Nations voted to divide the territory into Jewish and Arab nations. Jewish residents approved the plan. Arabs rejected it.

On May 14, 1948, Israel declared independence. The Arab nations of Egypt, Jordan, Syria, Lebanon, Iraq, and Saudi Arabia swiftly attacked the new country, pledging to secure the entire territory for the Palestinians. Israel beat back its enemies and, in the process, captured land that was supposed to be Palestinian. Once again displaced, the Palestinians were forced to flee to Jordan and Lebanon.

In 1967, Israel again found itself at war with its Arab neighbors. This time, the Jewish state captured the Gaza Strip from Egypt and the West Bank from Jordan—areas with large Palestinian populations. The Palestinians in these "occupied territories" were forced to carry identity cards and live under conditions much worse than did Jews in Israel. A generation of Palestinians has grown up with great bitterness under Israeli rule, vowing to defeat the occupiers at any cost.

Funding for the Palestine Liberation Organization (PLO) and other groups dedicated to waging war on Israel has come from numerous sources in the Middle East, notably Libya, Syria, and Iran. Sometimes, the terrorists engaged in spontaneous acts, like running through a marketplace, stabbing people. Other times, incidents were carefully planned to gain international attention, such as the 1973 murder of American and Belgian diplomats at a reception in the Sudan, or the 1975 seizure of eighty-one hostages at a meeting of oil ministers in Vienna, Austria.

The Palestinian terrorist network has never been united. Some groups were Communists who opposed religion,

Yasir Arafat, the recognized leader of the PLO, has publicly denied involvement in terrorist activities. He has long said that terrorist activities for which the PLO has taken credit were in fact sponsored by more radical splinter groups.

The World's Most Powerful Terrorist: Abu Nidal

Sabri al-Banna grew up a child of privilege, living in what would become the state of Israel. His father was a prosperous landowner and exporter, with a harem of thirteen wives. Family vacations were spent in Turkey, Egypt, and France.

But when Israel was founded in 1948, Sabri's family, like those of thousands of other Palestinians, lost everything. The fighting between Arabs and the new Jewish settlers eventually drove the Bannas into a refugee camp. There, the boy vowed to do whatever was necessary in the name of the Palestinian cause.

By 1964, Sabri al-Banna had taken the name Abu Nidal, meaning "Father of the Struggle." In the years to come he became the most notorious terrorist on earth, masterminding attacks throughout the Middle East and Europe. On one single day, December 27, 1985, Nidal's forces attacked two separate airports—in Vienna, Austria and Rome, Italy—with gunfire and grenades, killing seventeen and wounding one hundred.

Nidal gained much of his reputation as head of Fatah, the terrorist wing of the Palestine Liberation Organization (PLO). But his extreme positions put him out of favor with PLO leader Yasir Arafat. In the mid-1970s, Nidal's new Fatah Revolutionary Council was targeting Arafat, along with their mutual enemy, Israel.

Over time, Nidal had many sponsors—Iraq, Syria, and Libya, among them—providing money and documents necessary for his hit squads to travel from country to country. Eventually he came to be regarded as a terrorist for hire, willing to dispatch teams anywhere for the right price.

Additionally, Nidal became a master extortionist who, intelligence agents said, forced such governments as Austria, France, and Belgium to pay hefty fees to prevent terrorist activities on their soil.

Operating out of Libya—home to his terrorist training camps—Nidal's organization was, during the early 1990s, said to have between fifty and two hundred operatives working secretly around the world and one thousand sympathizers ready to assist them. The organization was also said to have a budget of $150 million.

The United States remained at the top of Nidal's hit list. "When we have the chance to do just the smallest harm to the Americans, we don't hesitate," he said in 1985. "It is a war of life and death between us and the Americans."

while others wished to create a new Islamic fundamentalist—or militantly religious—state, like Iran.

The historic peace agreement between Israel and the PLO, signed on September 13, 1993, opened the door to tranquility between Jews and Arabs in the Middle East. This agreement is a major step toward peace in the Middle East, but there is still much more work left to be done.

In recent years, the influence of Islamic fundamentalist groups has been growing, creating an especially dangerous situation. Already, many Palestinians have grown up in miserable conditions in the occupied territories, believing that there was little to live for. When these same people become fundamentalists, a few may be willing to sacrifice themselves for their cause. They think nothing of blowing themselves up in a crowd, for example, because they are convinced that they will be rewarded in the afterlife.

Chapter 3

Terror in Action

Devastating acts of violence have shown the world that terrorism threatens everyone.

Whether motivated by religion, politics, or a combination of both, terrorists have been responsible for some of the most dramatic—and tragic— events witnessed on the world scene in the past twenty-five years. Here's a look at some major instances of terror in action.

The Munich Olympic Massacre

A daring terrorist act took place in front of millions of television viewers over a twenty-three hour period on September 5, 1972, during the Olympic Games in Munich, Germany. An hour before dawn, eight invaders—carrying machine guns and hand grenades in athletic bags—scaled a chain-link fence and entered the Olympic Village, where the Israeli athletes were staying. Without notice, the group entered Building 31, lodging quarters for the Israeli Olympic team, and knocked on the door.

"I heard the knocking and then a terrible cry," said Israeli weightlifting coach Tuvia Sokolsky. "...Then I heard my friends yelling, 'Gct out! Escape!' I couldn't open the window, so I broke it and ran out."

Meanwhile, wrestling referee Yosel Gutfreud, weightlifter Yosef Romano, and wrestling coach Moshe Weinberg blocked the door, while some of their companions and the athletes from the other countries fled the

Opposite:
A member of an Arab commando unit steps onto the balcony of Building 31 during the siege of the Israeli Olympic team headquarters in Munich, Germany, September 1972.

Libyan leader Muammar el-Qadaffi has been a long-time supporter of terrorist activities around the world. Libya is also the home of the world's most active terrorist training camps.

building. The terrorists fired a machine gun through the door, killing Weinberg.

The Israelis were forced to stand in a cluster, back to back, while their bodies were tied together with ropes. The terrorists—members of the Black September group, named for the Palestinian commandos killed during a shootout with Jordanian troops in September 1970—rejected an offer by German officials to let the officials take the Israelis' place. The outlaws demanded the release of 200 comrades imprisoned in Israel and safe passage to the Middle East.

As the world watched, negotiations went back and forth. Finally, it was agreed that the hostages and their captors would be transported by three helicopters to an air base fifteen miles from the Olympic Village. Then, it was promised, the terrorists would be allowed to board a plane to Egypt.

But the German police made a tragic error. At the airport, snipers were lying in wait for four or five terrorists. Authorities hadn't realized there were eight. When four guerillas were visible on the airfield, the sharpshooters opened fire. This caused the Black September members to turn on the hostages. By the end of the episode, a total of eleven Israelis, five Palestinians and one German police-man were killed. Three other terrorists were arrested.

While most of the world condemned the attack, the government of Libya praised it. The five slain gunmen received heroes' funerals in the Arab country, with Libyan leader Muammar el-Qadaffi marching at the head of the procession. Then, in November, after the remaining three guerillas were flown to Libya in exchange for the release of a hijacked German airliner, the terrorists were greeted with wild cheers.

The Iranian Hostage Crisis

Iran was another nation harshly opposed to the West. From the moment he rose to power in February 1979, Iran's Islamic fundamentalist leader, the Ayatollah Ruhollah Khomeini, condemned America. America had supported the country's former dictator, Shah (or "King") Mohammad Reza Pahlavi, Khomeini said, and polluted Iranian minds with western influence.

"Our final victory will come when all foreigners are out of the country," Khomeini declared shortly after assuming control of Iran. "I beg God to cut off the hands of all evil foreigners and all their helpers."

The Americans staying at the U.S. embassy in the country's capital, Teheran, stood out as the symbol of the wicked strangers mentioned in Khomeini's speech. On November 4, 1979, about four hundred Iranian militants, calling themselves "students," began marching through Teheran's streets, proclaiming "death to America" and advancing on the embassy. When they arrived at the compound, the radicals cut through the chain-link fence and moved in. They received no resistance from the Iranian guards on duty. While staffers shredded sensitive documents, the U.S. Marines stationed at the facility fired tear gas canisters over the invaders' heads. But nothing could stop the mob. Everybody inside the building was eventually taken hostage.

For 444 days, America was forced to watch the Iranian militants humiliate their 52 captives (53 hostages were initially taken, but one man was released after 250 days) by forcing them to read anti-American statements on television and to march blindfolded in front of angry, chanting crowds. The revolutionaries claimed all the captives were spies, calling the embassy "a nest of vipers."

Negotiations went nowhere. Initially, the Ayatollah demanded that the Shah—who was receiving medical treatment in New York—be returned to Iran for "revolutionary justice." But after a while, it wasn't even clear if Khomeini had control of the people occupying the embassy, or if these "students" were simply acting on their own.

President Jimmy Carter admitted that the period was the "worst ever" of his administration. Americans were furious at their leader for being unable to stop a smaller and weaker country from making fools of the world's greatest superpower.

Even more damaging to Carter's administration was a botched effort to free the hostages. In April 1980, eight helicopters full of U.S. commandos were dispatched to

Iran's Ayatollah Khomeini endorsed the taking of U.S. hostages by Iranian students in 1979.

Iran to rescue the Americans. But the choppers were called back to base after three had technical failures. When the craft landed in the desert to refuel, one collided with a transport plane and eight servicemen were killed.

The disaster contributed to a growing American belief that Carter was a weak president. The following November, he was beaten by Ronald Reagan in a re-election bid. As a further blow to Carter, Khomeini's government waited until January 20, 1981—the day Reagan was inaugurated—to release the hostages.

A U.S. Army helicopter lies in a charred heap after a failed attempt to rescue the 52 American hostages held in Teheran, 1980.

Humiliation and Fear: Life as a Hostage

An American hostage during captivity in Iran.

From November 4, 1979, through January 20, 1981, the most prevalent topic of conversation in the United States was the hostage crisis in Iran. As a band of militants held fifty-two captives at the U.S. embassy in Teheran, Americans debated what could be done to free their fellow citizens.

In the embassy, the hostages knew little about the mood in the United States, although news periodically trickled in. Small bits of data—like information about several hostages' wives vigorously campaigning for their husbands' release—always inspired hope.

Early on in the siege, hostage Barry Rosen refused orders given by his captors. He was promptly marched outside, blindfolded. There, thousands of Islamic fundamentalists shouted at him, "The U.S. is our enemy!" and "Death to Carter!"—a reference to President Jimmy Carter. The message was clear: The captors were not an isolated group of fanatics; the hordes outside the embassy were ready to go to any extreme to support them.

If that wasn't terrifying enough, the militants frequently played games with their victims, suggesting that the undertaking was about to come to a violent finish. One bitterly cold night, hostage Moorehead Kennedy was awakened, dragged outside, and thrown against a wall. A gun was held to his back, and someone fired blank cartridges near his ear.

During visits to the bathroom, the hostages were forced to remain blindfolded. But they used those opportunities to scribble secret notes to one another on toilet paper. "Bathrooms were terribly important to us," Kennedy recalled. "A network of information went on through the bathroom."

When the crisis ended, life at home was a difficult adjustment—and proof that a hostage's problems don't end when freedom is granted. Within a year after returning to the United States, seven of the twenty-six married hostages separated from their spouses or filed for divorce. One man became a patient at a mental hospital.

The Lebanon Marine Compound Blast

At 6:22 a.m. on October 23, 1983, a yellow Mercedes truck passed through a Lebanese army checkpoint in the country's war-torn capital, Beirut, and headed toward the U.S. Marine compound. The American troops were part of a United Nations peacekeeping force sent to maintain order in a nation plagued by battles among competing militias. But the very presence of soldiers in U.S. uniforms on Lebanese soil infuriated Islamic fundamentalists who were resentful of American authority in the Arab world. Now, this driver was going to change the situation with one swift action.

Lance Corporal Eddie DiFranco was guarding the four-story headquarters, where most of the Americans were sleeping. Later, he wouldn't remember enough about the driver to provide a description. The only thing he could recall was "he looked right at me...and he smiled."

Outside the compound, the driver circled the parking lot, revved his engine, and smashed through the fence around the complex. The marine on duty in the guard shack realized that trouble was ahead. He raced from his post into the compound's lobby toward the rear entrance. "Hit the deck!" he shouted. "Hit the deck!"

Rescuers lower a U.S. Marine to safety after he was trapped in wreckage caused by a car bomb carrying twelve thousand pounds of dynamite. The car was driven by a member of the terrorist group Islamic Jihad.

At that very moment, the truck—carrying twelve thousand pounds of dynamite—crashed through the guard shack and into the lobby. The explosion that followed left a crater forty feet wide and nine feet deep. The guard was propelled into the air and out of the building. Most of the more than three hundred marines in the facility were not as lucky. Two-hundred-forty-one were killed in the blast, along with fifty-eight French peacekeepers.

There was no question that the driver—a member of the Islamic Jihad ("Islamic Holy War") terrorist group—was on a suicide mission to rid Lebanon of American troops. Despite the international outcry regarding his actions, he had accomplished his goal. American forces were pulled out of Lebanon not long afterward.

The TWA Hijacking

The Islamic Jihad was also behind the June 14, 1985, hijacking of TWA Flight 847. Ten minutes after the airplane took off from Athens, Greece, toward Rome, Italy, two men stood up and walked to the front of the aircraft. While one pulled out a nine-millimeter machine pistol and held it on the passengers, the other pushed a hand grenade into Flight Captain John Testrake's face and demanded he fly to Beirut.

As the plane headed toward the Middle East, the terrorists collected passengers' passports, forced them to sit in uncomfortable positions, and pistol-whipped anyone showing the slightest sign of hesitation. When there was some question about whether the craft would be allowed to land in Lebanon, one terrorist removed the pin from the hand grenade and threatened to blow himself up and everyone else on board if his orders weren't obeyed.

Among the terrorists' demands was the release of all members of their fellow Lebanese Shi'ite Muslims being held in Israeli prisons. The Shi'ites and Sunni Muslims are the two major sects of the Islamic religion.

In Lebanon, the plane refueled and seventeen women and two children were released. Then the jet was flown to Algeria, where another twenty-two passengers—mainly women and children—were set free.

Of the 113 remaining passengers, 104 were Americans. Since the hijackers considered America and Israel their enemies, passengers with Jewish-sounding last names and members of the U.S. armed forces were placed in a separate section of the plane. If anything went wrong, the terrorists warned, these would be the first travelers to be harmed.

Once again, the airplane flew toward Beirut. Again there was confusion over whether the aircraft could land. Plus, the terrorists wanted local Shi'ite Muslim leaders brought to the plane. If their demands were not met within two minutes, the hijackers threatened, an American would be killed.

Members of the Islamic Jihad hijacked TWA flight 847 in June 1985 and forced the pilot to fly to Beirut. In Beirut, the hijackers killed one American and held the other passengers hostage for seventeen days.

True to their word, the hijackers picked out U.S. Navy diver Robert Stethem, who had been badly beaten and was barely conscious. He was promptly shot in the head and killed. They would have killed another navy diver, Clinton Suggs, had flight attendant Uli Derickson not stepped in front of one of the gunmen, shouting, "Enough! Enough!"

From Lebanon, the plane returned to Algeria, then proceeded back to Beirut for a third time. There, Shi'ite leader Nabih Berri—acting as a mediator—persuaded the hijackers to hand over thirty hostages to his militia to hold until the matter was resolved.

But the crisis finally ended—seventeen days after it started—when America persuaded Syrian president Hafez al-Assad to help. It was well known that Assad sponsored terrorist activity all over the world, including Lebanon. But his intervention allowed him to show his competitors in that turbulent nation that he was the only one who could control a situation there. After his discussions with the heads of Lebanese terrorist groups, the American hostages were sent to Syria before they were safely flown to Germany.

One of the Beirut terrorists holds a gun to TWA pilot John Testrake during a live television broadcast.

Shi'ite leader Nabih Berri acted as a mediator to end the siege of TWA Flight 847 in June 1985.

The *Achille Lauro* Hijacking

On October 1, 1985, the *Achille Lauro,* an Italian cruise ship, set sail for Egypt and Israel. Among the 427 unsuspecting passengers and 80 crew members on board were four Palestinian terrorists traveling under false names with fake passports.

The original plan for the terrorists was to remain anonymous until the ship anchored in the Israeli port city of Ashdod. Once there, they would blow up oil storage tanks and an ammunition depot nearby. But the scheme was changed when, on the day the ship departed, Israeli jets attacked Palestine Liberation Organization (PLO) headquarters in Tunisia. This was the base the terrorists were supposed to periodically call for instructions. With communications now cut off, the terrorists panicked.

The Italian luxury liner *Achille Lauro* was overtaken by terrorists in October 1985. After ordering the captain to sail to Syria, the Palestinian terrorists shot a wheelchair-bound American and threw him overboard.

Believing they had been discovered, the intruders suddenly burst into the ship's dining room on October 7, machine guns and pistols blazing. Holding the entire vessel hostage, they ordered Captain Gerardo de Rosa to sail toward Syria.

If Israel didn't release fifty Palestinian prisoners, the terrorists threatened to kill the passengers one by one, starting with the Americans and British. One hostage, wheelchair-bound New Yorker Leon Klinghoffer, refused to be bullied. When the hijackers made a remark about the Jewish star around his neck, he insulted them back. For his defiance, Klinghoffer was killed and thrown overboard.

But the pirates realized this was a battle they couldn't win. When Egyptian president Hosni Mubarak offered them a chance to exit in Egypt and fly to PLO headquarters in Tunisia, they took it.

However, the United States could not tolerate the possibility of the terrorists getting away. American fighter planes intercepted the hijackers' flight in midair and forced it to land in Italy.

Unfortunately, the Italian government had not been informed about the U.S. operation. On the ground, Italian and American forces argued over which country

Supposed *Achille Lauro* hijacking ringleader Abul Abbas is escorted by Italian authorities during his trial. Although eleven terrorists were eventually convicted, Abbas was released.

had authority over the terrorists. So heated were the words that it seemed like the two units might fire on each other. Eventually, the United States relented, and allowed the Italians to take the pirates into custody.

Eventually, fifteen accused terrorists—including those who were said to have helped plan the operation—were tried in Italy, and eleven were convicted. But Americans were frustrated that the mastermind of the *Achille Lauro* hijacking, Abul Abbas, was released by Italian authorities and fled to the Middle East to plot other terrorist acts.

The Lockerbie Bombing

On December 21, 1988, Pan Am Flight 103 exploded over Lockerbie, Scotland, killing all 259 passengers on the plane and eleven people on the ground. Many of the passengers were Americans returning home for Christmas.

Terrorism was instantly suspected. Since the plane had departed from London, some were certain the IRA had planted the bomb. Others accused the numerous Palestinian gangs active in terrorism throughout the world. But a three-year investigation eventually led the United States government to blame the government of Libya.

Two Libyan officials, Abdel Basset Ali al-Megrahi and Lamen Halifa Fhimah, were charged with constructing the bomb in Malta, a nation in the Mediterranean Sea, packing it in a suitcase, and placing it on the flight where it originated in Frankfurt, Germany.

Their motive apparently was revenge for a 1986 attack by U.S. warplanes on Libya, which was in retaliation for a bomb placed in a German disco frequented by American military personnel. Two soldiers were killed.

The Lockerbie investigation began with agents collecting fragments from the blast scattered over 845 square miles of the Scottish countryside. Eventually, a small piece of plastic was traced to a radio, in which ten to fourteen ounces of plastic explosives had been hidden.

Using his position as a Libyan Arab Airlines employee in Malta, Fhimah was able to steal Air Malta labeling tags for the suitcase containing the bomb. On the morning of the discharge, Fhimah and Bassett placed the luggage on an Air Malta flight to Frankfurt, Germany. There, the suitcase was transferred to an airplane bound for London, then switched to Pan Am Flight 103, where it exploded.

The United States and Great Britain—which governs Scotland—demanded that Libya turn over the suspects for trial. In July 1992, the Libyan Parliament announced that the country would agree to hand over the men to either the United Nations or the Arab League—a coalition of Arab countries. However, American and British leaders insisted that the proceedings take place in one of their countries. Negotiations continued to drag on. As of October 1993, Libya said the two men could stand trial in Scotland if they wished, but no surrender date had been formally set.

In the wake of the tragedy, many asked the same question: Why weren't the terrorists stopped before they were able to strike?

Some of the wreckage of Pan Am Flight 103 lies in a field in Lockerbie, Scotland, after an explosion killed all the plane's passengers.

Chapter 4

Combating an Unseen Enemy

P utting an end to terrorist plots before they can be executed is a task that requires government investigators in the United States and elsewhere to draw on a wide variety of resources. An understanding of the techniques and weapons terrorists use is one resource. Another consists of sharing information on the activities of potentially hostile groups with other countries, establishing anti-terrorist communication networks. Using informants—terrorist insiders who provide secret information rather than go to jail—and, most of all, acting on that information at the right times, are also crucial to frustrating terrorists and saving lives.

Sophisticated technology and powerful weapons have made terrorists an even greater threat.

Weapons of Terror

Investigators—though they often know a lot about a terrorist's potential tools of destruction—must always be aware of all the things they don't know as well.

Opposite:
An FBI agent listens in on a wiretap during an anti-terrorist surveillance operation.

In the past, terrorists have used weapons that have evaded security. Plastic explosives, such as RDX and Semtex, can be carried through an airport metal detector, placed under the seat of an airplane, and set off with a small detonator or timer. The devices are small enough to be transported onto an aircraft in an envelope, or molded to look like shoe leather, clothesline, or Silly Putty.

Airplanes can be shot out of the sky at take-off with any number of grenade launchers, also capable of penetrating an armored car. Despite their firepower, these can be carried inconspicuously; in the late 1970s, American agents discovered a model of the SAM-7 anti-aircraft missile that could be placed in a suitcase. Rocket launchers from the former Soviet Union were favored by such diverse movements as Lebanese extremists and the IRA.

The Soviets were also responsible for designing the Kalashnikov assault rifle, used by revolutionaries since the end of World War II. While not always precise, the Kalashnikovs are considered sturdy and reliable. Other popular firearms are the Czech-made Skorpion VZ-61 and Israeli-manufactured Uzi, known for its light weight, small size, and effective rate of fire.

Plastic explosives are exceptionally light and can be hidden in many hard-to-detect places, like this book. Their use has increased the threat of terrorist bombings by offering a greater range of places in which to hide explosives.

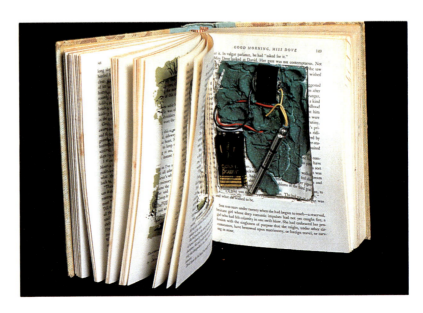

The disintegration of the Soviet Union left the newly independent republics with vast stocks of weapons originally intended for use against enemies backed by the United States. Because of the collapse of the economy in that region, people are desperate for cash. The black market for weapons and other battle materials has grown extremely large in the ex-Soviet Union because of these conditions. Today, a sizable portion of ex-Soviet weapons are available to anyone with enough cash to pay for them. Many organizations that battle terrorism worry that even nuclear weapons could fall into the wrong hands.

Cooperating with Former Enemies

The United States cannot work alone in the anti-terrorist efforts. Cooperation with other nations is essential. For years, America formed alliances with other countries to combat terrorism sponsored by the Soviet Union. However, with the collapse of the USSR, leaders in the Russian government now also worry about some of the same terrorist elements as the United States. Islamic fundamentalism, for example, is a threat to both countries. As a result, some surprising alliances have been formed. In June 1993, CIA director James Woolsey and Yevgeni Primakov, head of the Russian Foreign Intelligence Service—the successor of the KGB—met in Washington to discuss stopping terrorism, drug trafficking, and illegal arms shipments.

Uncovering the Plan to Kill George Bush

Close communication between the United States and Kuwait is credited with exposing a plan to murder former president George Bush during his visit to the Middle East in April 1993. Terrorists were said to have come up with three separate ways to eliminate Bush, who was being honored by the Kuwaitis for sending in American troops

In 1993, U.S. authorities uncovered an Iraq-backed plot to kill George Bush that had been planned for the ex-president's visit to Kuwait in April of that year. In retaliation, President Bill Clinton ordered an air strike against an Iraqi military facility and made it clear that America would not tolerate threats against its safety.

after the nation was invaded by Iraq in 1991. According to the plan, a remote-controlled car bomb would go off as the former president was entering the capital, Kuwait City. Another car bomb would detonate near a theater where Bush was receiving an award. And, if the two other attempts didn't work, a man wrapped in explosives would blow himself up to also kill the American leader.

Upon learning the terrorists' intentions, Kuwaiti officials said they arrested sixteen people, including eleven Iraqis, and confiscated high-tech equipment and hundreds of pounds of explosives. Kuwait alleged that Iraq was behind the plot.

In response to Iraq's involvement in the plot, President Bill Clinton launched an air strike on an Iraqi military facility, sending a signal around the world that America would use its armed forces to stop terrorism.

But recent events indicate that terrorists may be attempting to strike increasingly within the United States. Why? Do American immigration policies—relaxed compared to those of some other nations—allow foreigners with anti-American agendas to enter the country easily? Does the very nature of a democratic society mean that some citizens invariably abuse their freedom to harm others or further political causes that conflict with those of society at large? There are no clear answers. What is certain is that authorities have become more mindful of the fact that for the United States, terrorist trouble can begin at home.

Foiling American Nazis

The rise of racist skinheads, neo-Nazis, and other racist groups in America has the U.S. government on guard.

As of 1993, there were 3,500 racist skinheads in 40 states, compared to 1,500 skinheads in 12 states in 1988. Distributing material critical of blacks, Jews, gays, and Asians, these hostile gangs are commonly called "white supremacists" because they believe that whites are superior to other races. By 1993, groups such as these are already responsible for at least twenty-two known murders.

In July 1993, in Los Angeles, local police and federal agents arrested eight skinhead members of various white supremacist groups and charged them with a scheme to create racial turmoil in the United States. The skinheads' plan was to cause chaos all over the country and provoke

Groups of American racist skinheads are increasing. Similar to hate groups in Germany and England, skinheads often use violence to promote their ideas of white supremacy.

blacks and whites into fighting each other. According to their plan, a group of skinheads would invade one of Los Angeles's largest black churches, the First African Methodist Episcopal Church, firing machine guns directly at the congregation and murdering the pastor, the Reverend Cecil Murray. Other well-known blacks, such as the Reverend Al Sharpton, the rap group Public Enemy, and Rodney King—whose beating by Los Angeles police officers triggered riots in that city—would also be killed. The white supremacists hoped that blacks in communities everywhere would be so outraged that they would attack whites. Then, whites would feel justified in responding with equal violence.

The FBI investigation took eighteen months, during which time investigators worked undercover. An agent posed as a white supremacist and an informer pretended to be a minister of the Church of the Creator, a group combining racist and religious theories. Working undercover, they were able to sense that trouble was brewing.

A raid targeting suspects' homes took place before the alliance was about to send a letter bomb to an Orange County, California rabbi. Pipe bombs, machine guns, a confederate flag, a Nazi flag, and a framed portrait of Adolf Hitler were taken. FBI special agent Charlie Parsons told *Time* magazine that the government had to act before someone was hurt. "It was a judgment call that they might do something without telling us," he said. "These people are very unpredictable, and it's been like riding a bucking horse."

Uncovering the United Nations Bombing Conspiracy

An informant also proved useful in June 1993, when the FBI said that it foiled a plan by Islamic extremists—some linked to the bombers of the World Trade Center—to blow up the United Nations, two tunnels connecting New

York to New Jersey, and a government office building. Law enforcement officials also claimed the conspirators had planned to assassinate United Nations secretary General Boutros Boutros-Ghali, New York senator Alfonse D'Amato, and New York assemblyman Dov Hikind.

The informant was Emad Salem, a former Egyptian military officer who had served as a bodyguard for Sheik Omar Abdel Rahman, the Muslim preacher several of the bombing suspects followed. Salem's decision to help the

In June 1993, the FBI uncovered a large-scale terrorist plot to cause destruction throughout New York City. Among the attacks planned were bombings of the Holland and Lincoln tunnels, a government office building, and the United Nations headquarters, shown here.

Taping Terror

Before a raid can be conducted on a suspected terrorist group, investigators must first have ample evidence against the suspects. In the case against those who planned to destroy the United Nations, the government informant was said to have secretly made "highly incriminating" videotapes of the suspects, including one in which they were mixing chemicals for a bomb.

Pretending to be part of the conspiracy, the informant, Emad Salem, also recorded the following telephone conversation with defendant Siddig Ibrahim Siddig Ali:

Salem: Now, what is the purpose. . .[in] getting the United Nations? Are you out for a particular person or do you want to demolish the whole building? That would be another story, if this is the goal.

Ali: This is the world's government.

Salem: That's it. That's it.

Ali: Who governs the world today?

Salem: That is okay. That's it. Your idea about the United Nations is an excellent idea.

Ali: Now, we don't want to mention it by name. Let's agree on a code name.

Salem: Okay. Give it a name.

Ali: Any name...What about *Al-bait al-kabir* (Arabic for "the big house")?

government was supposedly based on his belief that terrorism hurt the Islamic religion and would cause hatred of Muslims all over the world. But critics of the investigation said that Salem's motive was purely financial; the FBI reportedly gave him $250,000 to assist them.

Apparently, the plotters trusted Salem so much that they picked him to make the explosives and rent the house that would be converted into the bomb factory. He was also put in charge of checking the house for hidden microphones.

At 1:30 a.m. on June 24, a team of New York City police officers and FBI agents stormed a garage in Queens, where five men were using wooden spoons to stir the contents of fifty-five-gallon barrels. Inside the barrels was a deadly "witch's brew"—as the FBI called it—a mixture of fertilizer and diesel fuel that formed an explosive paste.

Prosecutor Mary Jo White told the press that Siddig Ibrahim Siddig Ali, the supposed leader of the group, had been heard boasting, "We can get you anytime!" after the World Trade Center blast. "Law enforcement's answer is, 'No, you can't,'" she said. "We will not permit the likes of these defendants to terrorize our city."

Sheik Omar Abdel Rahman: Accused Ringleader

As information was released about the World Trade Center bombing and the plan to blow up the United Nations and other New York sites, one man's name was constantly mentioned. Sheik Omar Abdel Rahman, a blind, gray-bearded Islamic preacher, was frequently referred to as the spiritual leader of several terrorist plotters.

Sheik Omar Abdel Rahman has been identified by U.S. authorities as one of the major figures in a New Jersey ring of terrorist plotters. The sheik and his followers have been linked to the World Trade Center bombing as well as the plot to blow up the United Nations and murder several New York political leaders.

Anti-Arab Prejudice

Shortly after the World Trade Center bombing, Hamid Kherief, a professor at New York's LaGuardia Community College, left his home, dressed in a traditional Muslim tunic.

A passing driver shouted out the window, "What are you? Abouhalima?"

The reference was clear. Because Kherief was a Muslim, the driver was quick to associate him with World Trade Center suspect Mahmud Abouhalima. To Kherief, it seemed that too many non-Muslims believe that everyone who follows Islam is somehow linked to terrorist activities.

Mahmud Abouhalima was one of the suspects connected to the bombing at the World Trade Center.

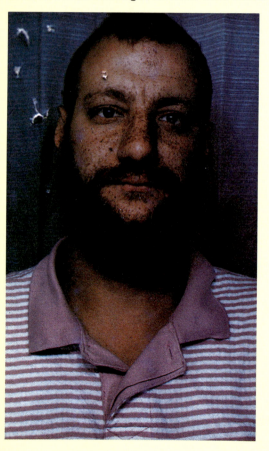

"I haven't worn it again," the professor said of his tunic. "People stop seeing you as an individual when they see that kind of attire."

Ahmed Hasheem understands those feelings. The Egyptian worshipped at the same mosque as Abouhalima, and was manager of Hungry Hamed's, a gathering spot for local Arabs. But when he opened a restaurant of his own, there was no suggestion of his heritage in the name or decorations. Hasheem called the place "Zurich Chicken" after the Swiss city. The interior was adorned with the same Formica tiles and fluorescent lights found at most shopping malls. Hasheem told the newspaper *New York Newsday*, that he had specifically made it a point to operate a business "without a trace of Islam on the walls."

With incidents like the World Trade Center bombing receiving so much publicity, American Muslims take these precautions not out of shame, but fearing their neighbors' violent reactions. "There's a sense of dread, an enormous stress on our community," explained Jim Zogby, president of the Arab-American Institute, a Washington, D.C.-based organization that is devoted to bettering the lives of Arab Americans.

There are between six- and eight-million Muslims in the United States. They come from Middle Eastern countries like Jordan, Syria, and Yemen; Asian nations like the Philippines, Thailand, and Indonesia; as well as Africa, Europe, and the Caribbean. In fact, only 12.4 percent of all American Muslims are Arabs. The majority—42 percent—are African Americans.

Islam is America's fastest-growing religion, and most followers have never been in trouble with the law. Yet, when a small percentage are accused of terrorist acts, all members of the religion feel some type of prejudice.

"Radicals are radicals, and every group has them—Catholics, Jews, skinheads, Muslims," said Joseph Govlick, a New Jersey attorney who has several Muslim clients. "The problem is that radicals make up a tiny part of the community, and the media blows things so far out of proportion that the entire Muslim community becomes suspect."

According to one surveillance tape, the sheik told some of the suspects, "American blood should be spilled on its own soil."

In his native Egypt, Abdel Rahman found himself at odds with the country's leaders, who enjoyed good relations with the West. He criticized tourists for visiting such "pagan" monuments as the pyramids, instead of Muslim shrines, and for bringing corrupt values to the Middle East.

When Egyptian president Anwar el-Sadat made peace with his former enemy, Israel, he was harshly criticized by fundamentalists. In 1981, he was assassinated by extremists while watching a parade. The sheik went on trial for encouraging the execution, but was found innocent.

In 1990, Abdel Rahman went to the American embassy in Khartoum, the capital of Sudan, and was granted a visa to visit the United States as a tourist. Later, U.S. officials would claim they had made a mistake in issuing the visa, because the sheik was already listed as a terrorist.

But some insist that the CIA knew all about the sheik, and was rewarding him for helping U.S.-supported guerillas wage war against the Soviet-controlled government of Afghanistan in the 1980s. Like the sheik, the guerillas were Islamic fundamentalists. However, they shared the same enemy with the United States at the time: the Soviet Union.

From mosques in New York and New Jersey, Abdel Rahman continued to condemn the West, and tapes of his sermons were smuggled back to followers in the Middle East. It soon became unclear whether the sheik would be allowed to remain in the United States. As more facts about terrorist plots were uncovered, the pressure grew to remove or punish the sheik for his involvements. On August 26, 1993, Abdel Rahman was charged—along with fourteen co-defendants—with being a part of the group that was responsible for the World Trade Center bombing.

Chapter 5

Fearing the Future

Terrorism is as much a mental as a physical ordeal. One year after being beaten by the hijackers of TWA Flight 847—and watching them murder his friend, Robert Stethem—U.S. Navy diver Clinton Suggs was still afraid to board an airplane. Said his wife, "Clint is a very different person now. It's been a very bad year."

Kurt Carlson, a major in the military reserve, was beaten for four-and-a-half hours during his captivity. "I am a trained combat soldier, but I learned that you need something else to survive. It's faith and prayer that keeps you going."

But he was quick to add, "I don't think you ever get over something like this."

Containing the Plague

The potential for terrorism today is greater and more widespread than it has been in the past. In the Arab world, numerous nations that have sponsored terrorism are now competing for domination of the Middle East. In Latin America, revolutionary organizations—like Shining Path in Peru—are said to receive funding from drug trafficking, among other activities. (Although Shining Path founder Abimael Guzman was captured by a special Peruvian anti-terrorist squad in 1992, the organization still exists.) The aim of the Shining Path is to achieve equality for rural peasants through revolution. Organizers of this

As the threat of terrorism grows, personal freedoms and conveniences may be sacrificed for safety.

Opposite:
Soon after taking office in 1993, President Bill Clinton asked his top advisers to explore new ways in which America could crack down on terrorist activities.

group focus their attention on urban areas and destabilize the government by blowing up electric power stations, roads, and bridges, and engaging Peru's army in battle.

What can a government do to protect its citizens? President Bill Clinton has asked his advisers to explore ways to tighten immigration requirements as a means of preventing those with terrorist backgrounds from moving to the United States. His overriding concern, according to his aides, is that terrorist threats will change America into a different type of nation, one in which residents will always "live in fear."

If known terrorists do find their way into the country, counterterrorist experts advise close surveillance. This approach, though, disturbs many Americans who believe that a democracy should not monitor the behavior of its citizens.

Workers at the FBI fingerprint headquarters in Washington, D.C., use highly sophisticated equipment to help investigators track down and capture known terrorists and their conspirators.

"In an open society like ours, there's absolutely nothing the government can do to stop terrorists," Eric Hammel, author of a book on the 1983 marine barracks bombing in Lebanon, told *Newsweek* magazine. "People aren't going to put up with a lot of checks and searches. That's not how Americans operate."

Debating the Media's Role

Americans generally don't approve of censorship, either. Yet, government officials have long insisted that media interviews of terrorists only serve as much-desired publicity for them.

In 1986, the NBC television network was accused of being "an accomplice to terror" for running an interview with Abul Abbas, the alleged mastermind of the *Achille Lauro* hijacking. Robert Oakley, head of the State Department's counterterrorism unit, said, "When a media outlet makes deals with a terrorist not to divulge his whereabouts, (it) is saying... 'We've become his accomplices in order to give him publicity.'"

In England, IRA supporters have been largely banned from appearing on television. But journalists and other defenders of free speech have argued that if the group couldn't state its position to the media, its only means of gaining attention would be bombing.

In societies with less freedom, anyone openly criticizing the government is arrested or deported. Censorship opponents in the United States point out that, rather than muffling terrorist ideas, this assault on liberty has actually inspired anti-government violence.

Using Diplomatic Muscle

Shortly after the plot to blow up the United Nations and other New York landmarks was uncovered, *U.S. News & World Report* claimed that the suspects were assisted by two officials posted at the Sudan's mission to the United Nations. According to the report, these individuals were going to help smuggle explosives into the United Nations building. But there was little the United States could do, since—under the terms of a special privilege called "diplomatic immunity"—foreign diplomats in the United States cannot be prosecuted for crimes.

Some people have suggested changing this law when the charge is terrorism. Others have said that nations sponsoring violence against U.S. citizens must be singled out and isolated. This means joining with other democracies to cut off aid and trade to these countries. At the same time, all the money these nations keep in American banks would be frozen. The money could not be withdrawn until the situation changed.

Calling in the Troops

On June 7, 1981, Israeli F-4 phantom jets breezed over the Iraqi capital of Baghdad and bombed a nuclear reactor under construction. The action was criticized around the world. After all, Israel had sent its air force into a foreign country and attacked without being provoked. But Israel insisted it was only protecting itself. Iraq had threatened to destroy the Jewish homeland on many occasions, Israeli officials said, so the potential for a nuclear attack had to be eliminated.

Ten years later, when Iraq fired missiles into Israel during the 1991 Persian Gulf War, many Israelis remembered and were grateful for the Baghdad raid. And many Americans were saying the United States should conduct similar attacks on terrorist spots around the world, destroying stockpiles of weapons, bombing training facilities, and storming houses used by guerillas. If terrorists think they can target anyone anywhere, the argument goes, then the United States should make them understand that they can never hide either.

An example of this attitude was the American missile assault on an Iraqi military facility in reaction to the country's plot to assassinate former president George Bush. Terrorist deeds are acts of war, the United States reasoned, and the volley of missiles was the appropriate retaliation.

How Safe Are the World's Airports?

What will it take to secure airports from terrorism? Experts believe the answer lies in perfecting devices capable of detecting bombs, improving surveillance of terminals, and creating a computer system that contains detailed information about passengers with terrorist ties.

The Pan Am Flight 103 explosion revealed two major gaps in airport security: It is easy to check a bag onto a flight you may not board, and plastic explosives can easily pass through detectors.

For several years, numerous bomb-detection devices have been in development, including the "vapor sniffer," which can spot explosives by their scent rather than by their composition or shape.

Also, investigators advise that security guards should be better paid and better trained. A 1991 study found that some guards had as little as eight hours of instruction—an extremely ineffective amount of time, considering the creative techniques of most international terrorists.

If security is going to drastically improve, travelers must be willing to endure greater inconveniences at airports. Lines will be longer as security is tightened, and more luggage will be searched by hand. But counterterrorism experts insist that slower service is a worthwhile sacrifice when lives are at stake.

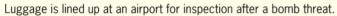

Luggage is lined up at an airport for inspection after a bomb threat.

What Individuals Can Do

As recent events show, no one can ever be completely safe from terrorism. But it is important for individuals to be aware of terrorist patterns in order to ensure safety when traveling or when in public spaces. Since terrorists frequently focus on airports and public areas, people are advised to follow the following rules when in these areas:

• At airports, avoid ticket counters, baggage check-in, and baggage claim areas as much as possible. These are the spots most often picked by terrorists for destruction.

• In public places, do not sit near trash cans, rest rooms, or other places where bombs can be planted. Avoid sitting near windows, which can shatter.

• Keep away from abandoned bags, briefcases, or packages. Inform security or police about any unclaimed or unattended items.

• At airports, never carry packages for strangers. Watch your bags closely to make sure that nobody inserts anything into them.

• If you notice anyone suspicious, inform the authorities. It never hurts to be too cautious. The more people willing to speak up and fight terrorism, the harder it will be for terrorists to be successful.

Still, even if airports were completely terrorist-proof, advocates of any given cause would find another way to create trouble. Despite new technologies, cooperation between friendly governments, and increased training of anti-terrorist forces, terrorism has become a feature of modern life that will be difficult to completely eliminate anytime in the near future.

Chronology

May 14, 1948	Israel declares its independence from Palestine. War erupts in the Middle East.
1970s	The Baader-Meinhof gang (later the Red Army Faction) commits a series of bombings and murders.
March 12–28, 1970	The Weathermen bomb office buildings and a night club in New York City. Three members are killed when explosives accidentally go off in Greenwich Village.
January 20, 1972	British troops kill 13 men involved in a protest. Known as "Bloody Sunday," this day rallies Irish Catholics' wrath.
September 1972	At the Olympic Games in Munich, Germany, Israeli athletes are held hostage by the terrorist group Black September. In the end, seventeen are killed.
December 29, 1975	The FALN is suspected in a bombing at La Guardia Airport in New York that kills twelve.
June 14, 1977	Using guns and demanding Croatia's freedom, three militant Croatians gain entrance into Yugoslavia's mission to the United Nations.
1978	Italy's Red Brigades kidnap and hold politician Aldo Moro for forty-five days. He is put on trial and later killed.
1979	The IRA murders Earl Mountbatten and attacks a British regiment, killing eighteen.
1979–1981	Fifty-two hostages are held by Iranian militants for 444 days.
1980s	Muammar el-Qaddafi begins training terrorists in Libya.
October 23, 1983	The U.S. Marine compound in Beirut, Lebanon is bombed by the Islamic Jihad. Over two hundred are killed.
June 14, 1985	TWA Flight 847 is hijacked by members of the Islamic Jihad and forced to fly to Beirut several times. One American is killed.
October 7, 1985	The Italian cruise liner *Achille Lauro* is hijacked by Palestinian terrorists who demand the release of fellow countrymen being held by Israel.
December 21, 1988	Plastic explosives are detonated on Pam Am Flight 103. Libya has its revenge for U.S. warplane attack—259 are killed.

1991	The Soviet Union dissolves. Regional and ethnic conflicts erupt through terrorism.		hostages are taken and a person is killed.
February 26, 1993	Terrorist bombing kills six at Two World Trade Center.	**July 1993**	Police and federal agents arrest skinhead members of white supremacist groups in Los Angeles. They are charged with scheming to create racial turmoil in America.
April 1993	An Iraq-backed plot to assassinate former president George Bush during his visit to the Middle East is discovered by Kuwait.	**September 13, 1993**	A peace agreement is signed between Israel and the PLO.
June 1993	Turkey's Kurdish minority terrorizes Turkish embassies and businesses in Europe—	**October 1993**	Four people go on trial for World Trade Center bombing.

For Further Reading

Kronenwetter, Michael. *United They Hate: White Supremacists in America*. New York: Walker & Co., 1992.

Landau, Elaine. *Terrorism: America's Growing Threat*. New York: Lodestar, 1992.

Lawson, Don. *America Held Hostage: From the Teheran Embassy Takeover to the Iran-Contra Affair*. New York: Franklin Watts, 1982.

Meyer, Carolyn. *Voices of Northern Ireland: Growing up in a Troubled Land*. San Diego, CA: Harcourt Brace, 1987.

Raynor, Thomas P. *Terrorism*. New York: Franklin Watts, 1982.

Index

63

Photo Credits

Cover: A. Borrel/Gamma-Liaison; pp. 4, 9, 16, 19, 21, 22, 26, 28, 30, 31, 32, 33, 35, 36, 37, 41, 51: AP/Wide World Photos; p. 6: ©S. Hirsch/Gamma-Liaison; p. 12: ©Steve Lock/Gamma-Liaison; pp. 14, 38: Gamma-Liaison; p. 39: P. Guerrini/Gamma-Liaison; p. 42, 59: Dirck Halstead/Gamma-Liaison; p. 44: ©Ruau-Figaro/Gamma-Liaison; p. 46: ©Gustavo Ferari/Gamma-Liaison; p. 47: ©John Berry/Gamma-Liaison; p. 49: ©Blackbirch Press; p. 52: ©Jon Levy/Gamma-Liaison; p. 54: B. Markel/Gamma-Liaison; p. 56: Terry Ashe/Gamma-Liaison.